The Kitten Psychologist

THEA VAN DIEPEN

Find other works by the author at
https://www.theavandiepen.com

The Kitten Psychologist

INKLETS #3

THEA VAN DIEPEN

Inkprint PRESS

www.inkprintpress.com

ISBN: 978-1-925825-03-9
eBook ISBN: 9781386437086

www.inkprintpress.com

*National Library of Australia Cataloguing-in-Publication
Data*
Van Diepen, Thea
The Kitten Psychologist
24 p.
ISBN: 978-1-925825-03-9
Inkprint Press, Canberra, Australia
1. Fiction—Animals 2. Fiction—Short Stories

First Print Edition: February 2019
Cover design © Inkprint Press
Interior art © Amy Laurens

THE KITTEN PSYCHOLOGIST

THERE ONCE WAS A LITTLE KITTEN WHO had decided that the outside was bad. One hundred percent, unequivocally, without question or shadow of a doubt, dangerous.

"I mean, why else," said the kitten, purring and cleaning its paws, "would we live in houses?"

But, alas, one day, the kitten's humans took it outside. Carried it right out the door.

"It was terrible," the kitten told me over Skype after the event. "One hundred percent, unequivocally, without question or shadow of a doubt, terrible. There was snow. It was cold and wet and it stuck in my fur. My humans laughed at me when they put me down and I refused to move."

Of course, I thought the kitten was being unreasonable. "Your ancestors lived outside. I'm sure they loved the snow. You should try it again."

"Your ancestors grew crops along the Volga River," the kitten pointed out. "Are you planning on trying that anytime soon?"

Darn kitten had a point.

I tried a different tack. "There's all kinds of things you can do outside that you can't do inside."

"Oh, sure, catch diseases, fall on ice, get attacked by wild animals or drunk drivers, and then die. Although I suppose you could still die inside." It flicked its tail thoughtfully.

"Dying without having ever left your house. That's depressing."

"Fruit flies do it all the time." The

kitten's eyes widened. "That *is* depressing."

"See?"

"Then I'll just live a long and healthy life inside and, when I'm dying, I'll have my humans take me outside where I can be with nature and junk. There. Problem solved." The kitten glared at me before being scooted off the desk by its human, who had returned to continue our conversation.

I was then able to follow the cat's activities using my arcane writerly powers.

Over the next few days, it would approach the doors and look out windows whenever it thought its humans weren't looking.

But they were. They told me about their kitten's change in behaviour, wondering aloud whether they should let it outside again.

It was at this point they also showed me the Youtube video of their kitten standing indignantly in the snow. I have to admit, it was pretty funny.

Not long after, the kitten called me up on Skype.

"You know, I've been thinking," it said.

"Really? And how did that make you feel?" I adjusted my imaginary spectacles and picked up my imaginary clipboard.

"Shut up. I'm trying to talk." The kitten stuck out its wee pink tongue and I couldn't help but laugh, at which point the kitten glared.

"Sorry, continue."

"I will. As I was saying, I've been thinking. About the outside. At first I was thinking, you know, I'm only a few weeks old. I've got a lot of life left in me. I really could just go out there and try out this whole snow thing again, or I could stay inside for a while. There's lots of time. But then I thought, do I really have as much time as I think? I could die at any moment. The fridge could fall over when I'm trying to open it and squash me, or I could get my tail stuck in an electrical outlet. Someone could be too curious in my vicinity. You know."

I nodded.

"And what if I don't die like that? What if I spend my whole life just staring at the outside instead of prancing out there and just owning it like cats should? What if all I do, for the rest of my life, is wait? I mean, it's not like there's anything stopping me from going outside. There's just... me."

"Sounds like you've made some important progress."

"But what if my humans laugh and take videos of me again?"

I took this moment not to mention that I'd both seen and laughed at the video.

Instead, I gave my most thoughtful face. "So, what you're trying to say is, you would rather go outside without them?”

The kitten stretched before answering. “I’ll admit, they’re much better as servants than they are as escorts. But they do happen to be able to reach doorknobs. Don’t they make doors in more cat-friendly sizes?”

“Yes,” I said. *They’re called doggy doors,* I thought, but didn’t say.

“Excellent.” The kitten purred. “I want one. Just for the backyard. I needn’t parade myself before the general public just yet.”

“I’ll mention it to your humans.” I suppressed a snigger at the phrase. “I’m sure they’ll listen to me.”

“Of course they’ll listen to you. What else have I been paying you for?” With that, the kitten hung up.

I’ve really got to tell my friends where their money’s been going.

Meh. I can wait until they get their next bank statement.

THE MAKING OF
THE KITTEN PSYCHOLOGIST

One day, in considering what to write to my email list, I had the idea to write about a kitten scared of going outside. Because snow. And dignity.

In true Thea fashion, this wasn't entirely about a kitten.

At the time, I was having a hard time figuring out what I was doing with my life, and resisting stepping out into new things. So. Well. I got to write about myself. As the kitten.

But I also figured, as I have a psychology degree, I could write myself into the story as a psychologist. It didn't quite turn out that way, as I seem to have ended up being in both the psychologist and the kitten and neither of them are exactly me... but it ended up being a rather wonderful therapy session with myself.

It took a bit of thought once I got close enough to the end, with no idea how to conclude it (a common occurrence in, well, any story I write). I sat and stared at the computer screen for a bit, trying to work it out until something slipped into place and there. There it was. The ending. And it was perfect.

DOWNLOAD YOUR FREE EBOOK

When you buy a print book from Inkprint Press, we like to say THANK YOU by offering you the ebook for free!

Please head to www.inkprintpress.com/inklets/3/ and the use the coupon INKLET3 to get your copy of this Inklet in epub AND mobi today!
(Coupon will only work once.)

READ MORE!

DREAMING OF HER AND OTHER STORIES

A collection of short stories and poetry, written as refreshers, reminders of what makes life beautiful. Pieces include a story of the life of a river as he discovers his true self, a poetic retelling of Daphne's flight from Apollo, and, in the titular story, a literal nightmare as a girl comes to terms with the death of her sister.

https://www.theavandiepen.com

ABOUT THE AUTHOR

THEA VAN DIEPEN spent the first ten years of her life on a tree-wrapped acreage where an inquisitive child might believe in magic. Nowadays, she lives in Edmonton, breathing life into stories in the form of books such as the *White Changeling* series, a webcomic, and a video game.

Her website is theavandiepen.com, where she can be contacted in English and French... so long as you don't ask her to count in French, as she tends to miss numbers ending in six entirely by accident.

INKLETS

Collect them all! Released on the 1st and 15th of each month.

SEVENTY
LIANA BROOKS

A Final Request
for Mercy
AMY LAURENS

the kitten psychologist
vs.
the kitten's owners
THEA VAN DIEPEN

Answer the
Question
AMY LAURENS

Happily
Red
AMY LAURENS

the kitten psychologist
tries to be patient
through email
THEA VAN DIEPEN

DRAGON
Tuesday
AMY LAURENS

RED PLANET
REFUGEES
LIANA BROOKS

the kitten psychologist &
What The Kitten Did
THEA VAN DIEPEN

Cherry Blossom
AMY LAURENS

Alone
AMY LAURENS

the kitten psychologist
& The Kitten
Come To A Conclusion
THEA VAN DIEPEN

LEVEL NINE
LIANA BROOKS

To Dust
AMY LAURENS

Interchange
AMY LAURENS

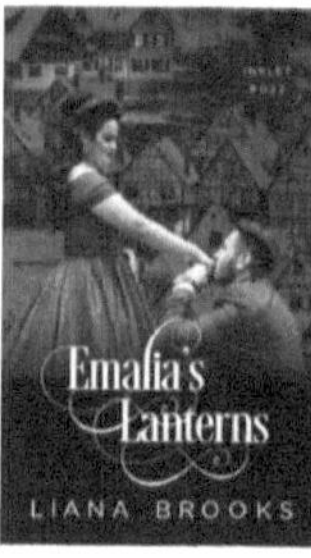
Emalia's
Lanterns
LIANA BROOKS

Dear Santa
AMY LAURENS

The
Quilt-Maker's
Scrap
AMY LAURENS